W9-CBG-668

Lineberger Memorial
Library
Donated by
Marilyn Stauffer
Lutheran Theological Southern Seminary Columbia, S. C.

FEET!

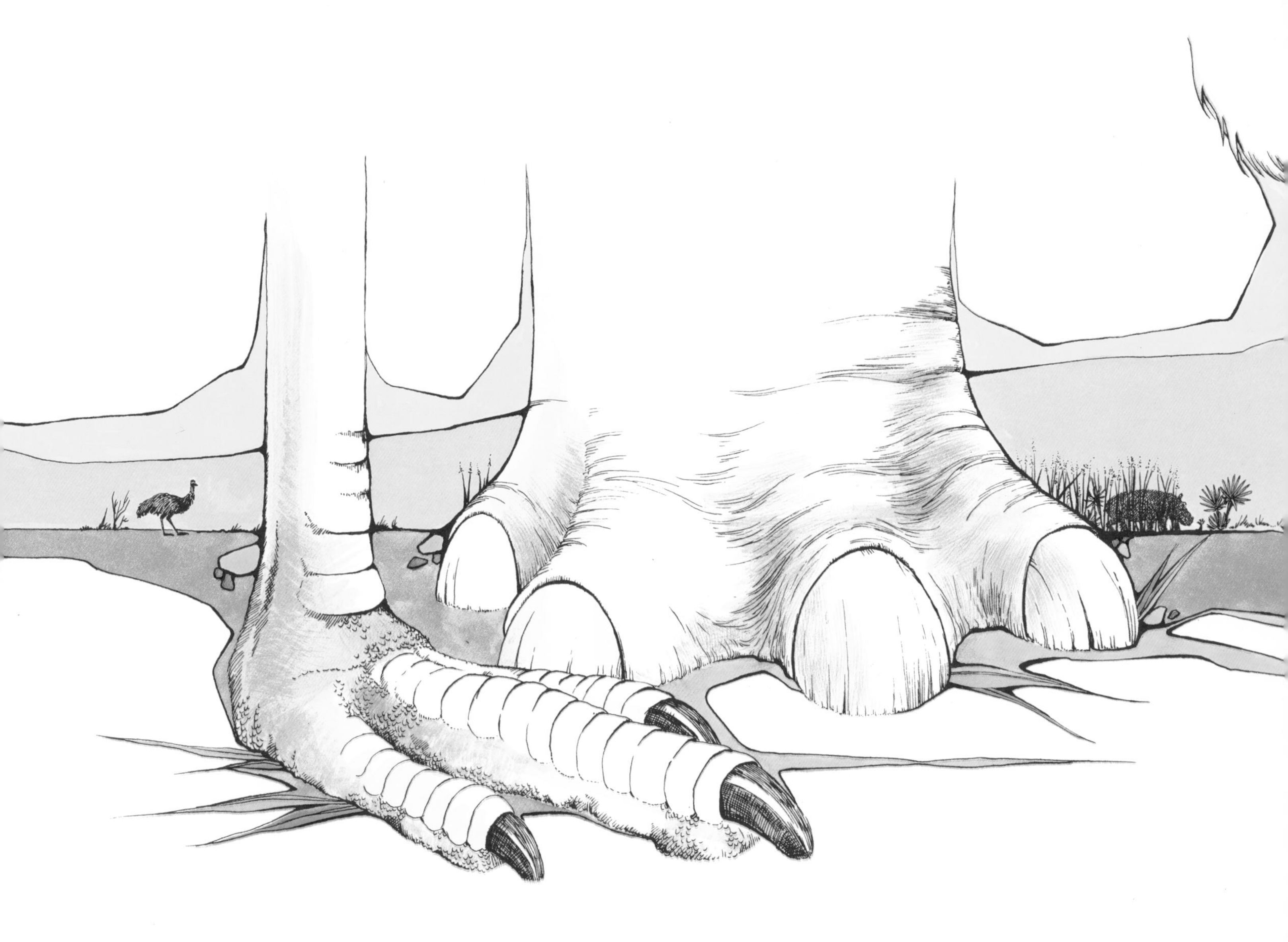

FEET!

WRITTEN AND ILLUSTRATED BY

PETER PARNALL

Macmillan Publishing Company New York

Collier Macmillan Publishers London

Macmillan Publishing Company, 866 Third Avenue, New York, NY 10022.
Collier Macmillan Canada, Inc. Printed and bound in Japan. First American Edition.
10 9 8 7 6 5 4 3 2 1
The text of this book is set in 24 point Baskerville. The illustrations are rendered in pen and ink and watercolor.
Library of Congress Cataloging-in-Publication Data • Parnall, Peter. Feet!
Summary: Looks at a variety of animal feet, from big feet and fast feet to cool feet and webbed feet. [1. Foot – Fiction. 2. Animals – Fiction] I. Title.
PZ7.P243Fe 1988 [E] 88-5272 ISBN 0-02-770110-7

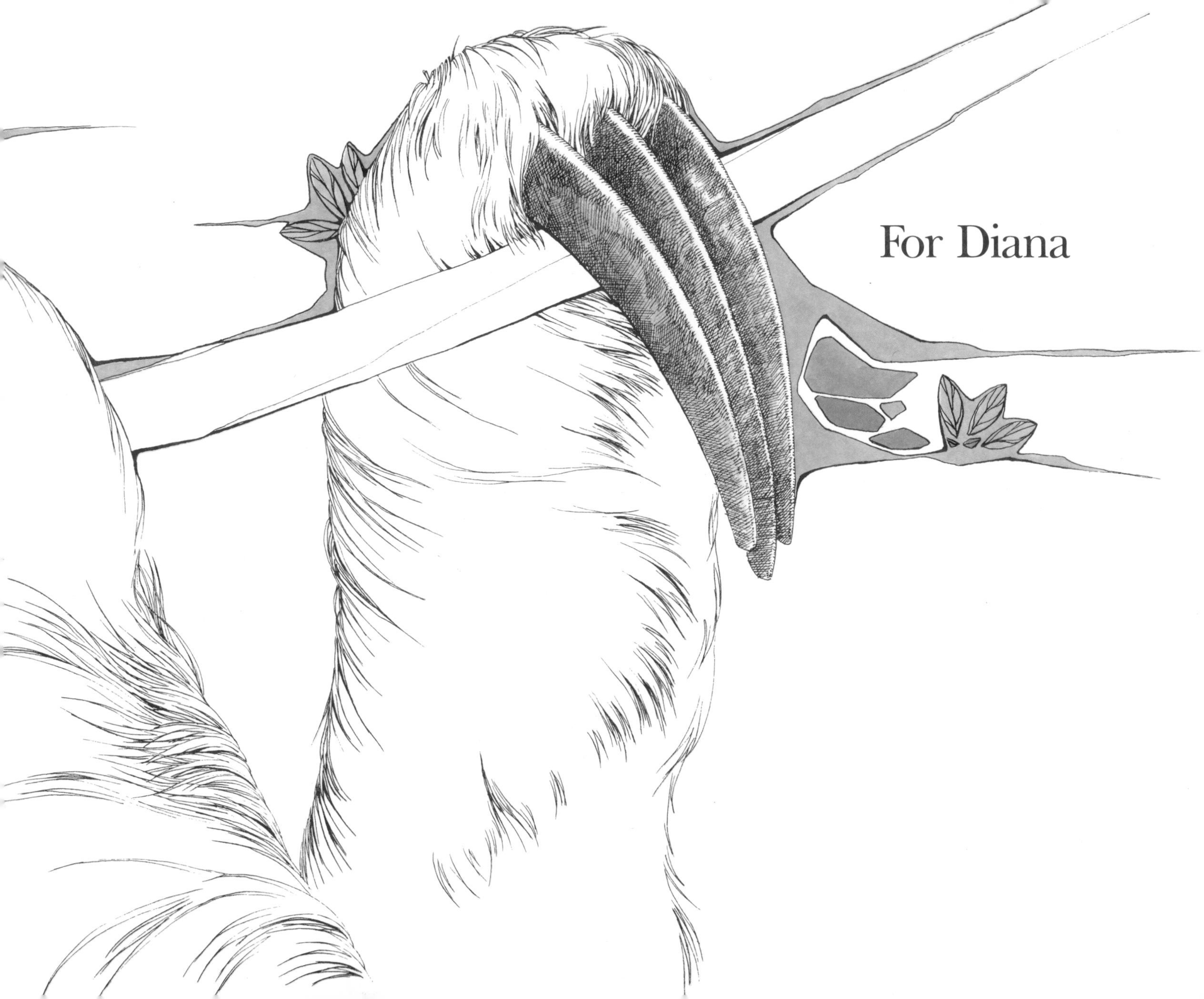

For Diana

I like **BIG** feet,

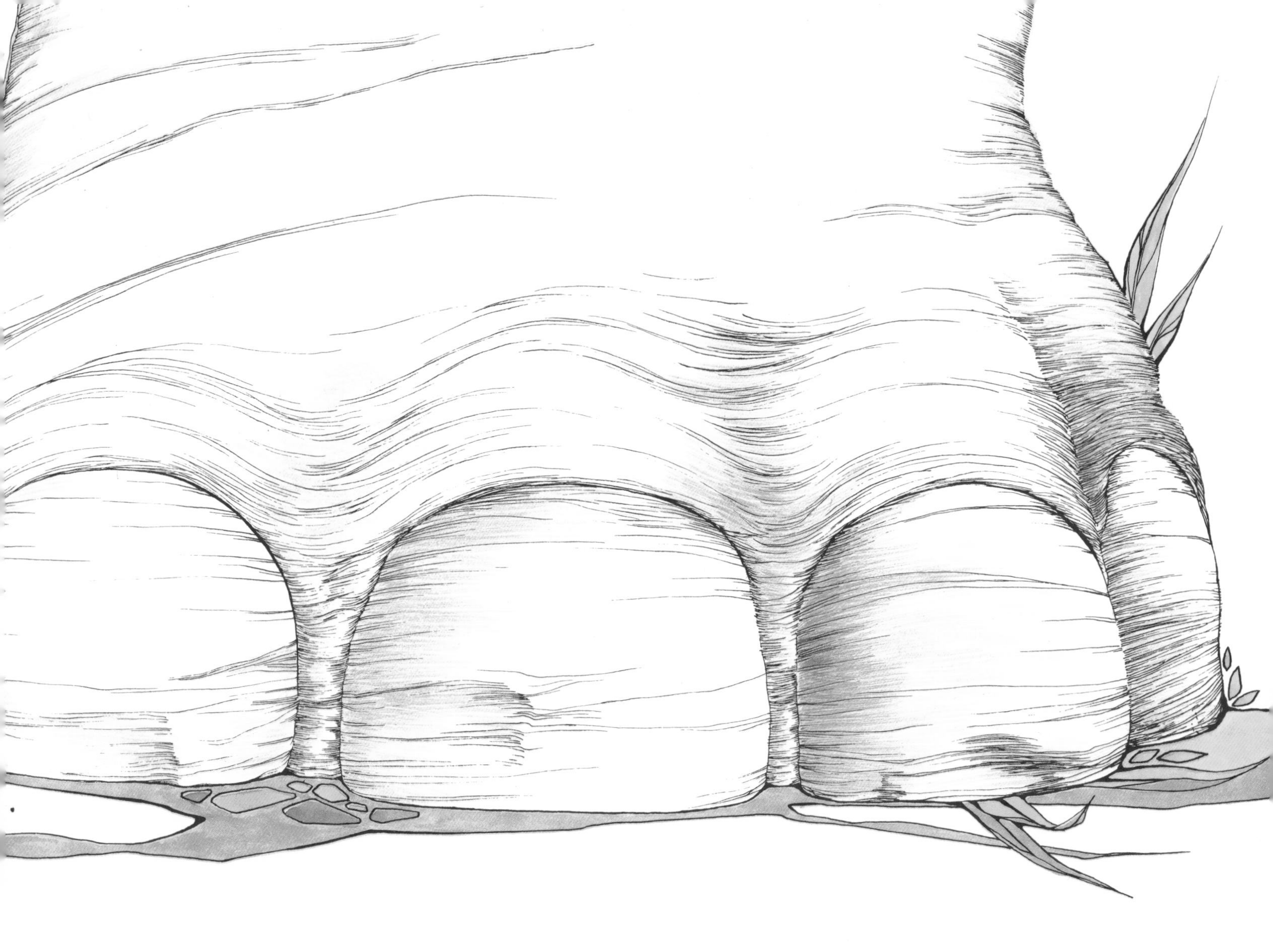

FAST feet,

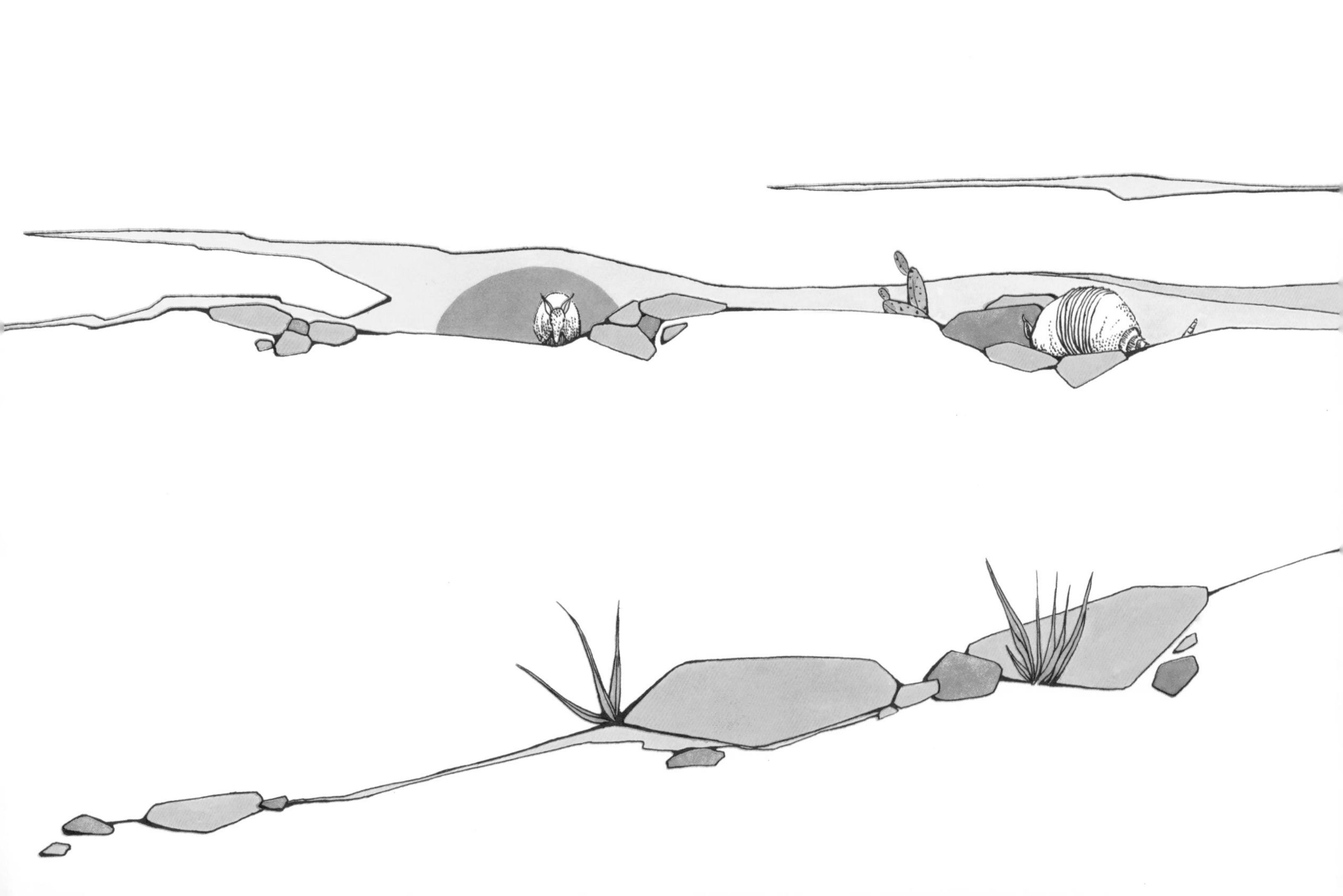

and LONG-TOED
SCALY feet.

I like

HAIRY feet,

TOUGH feet,

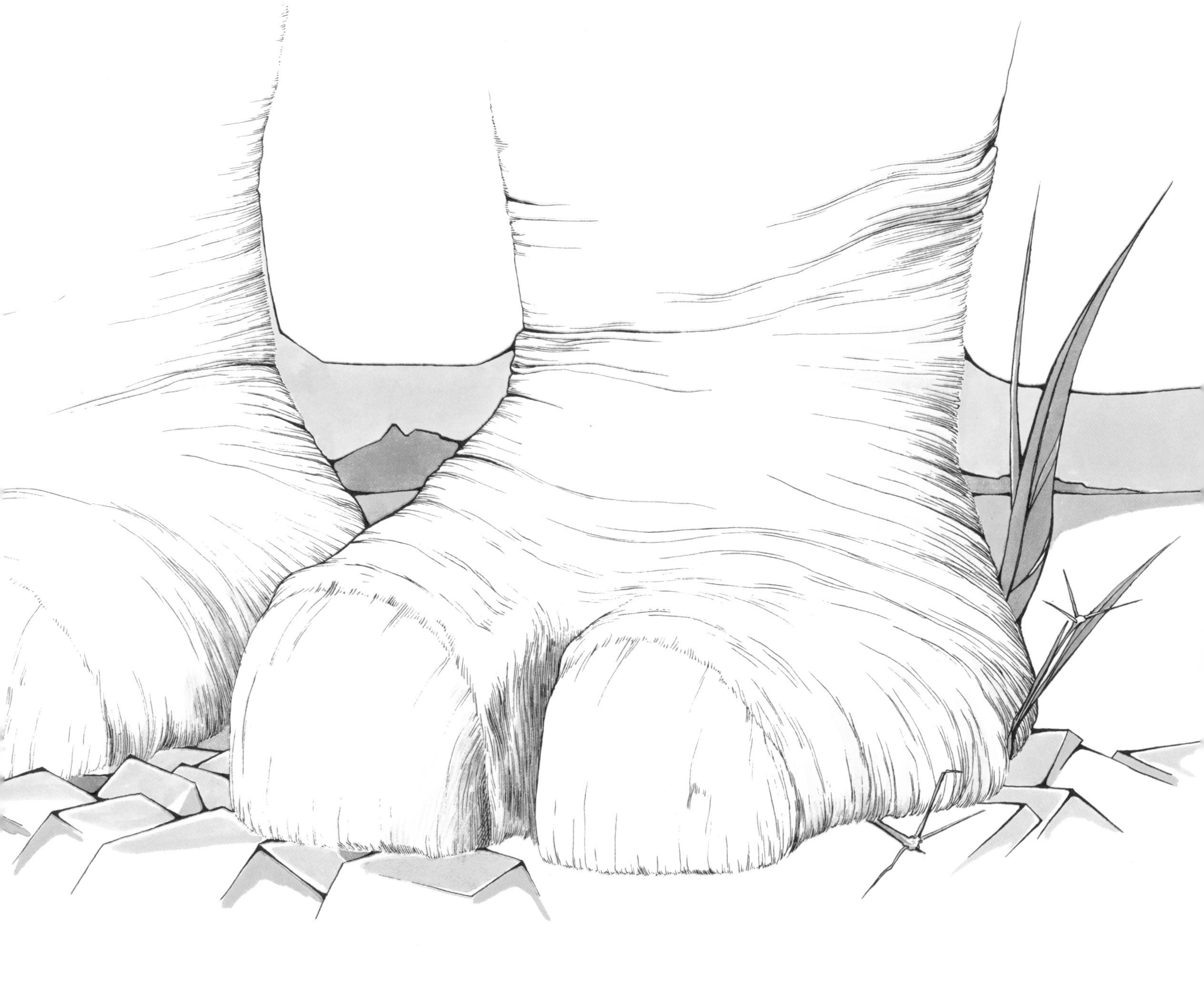

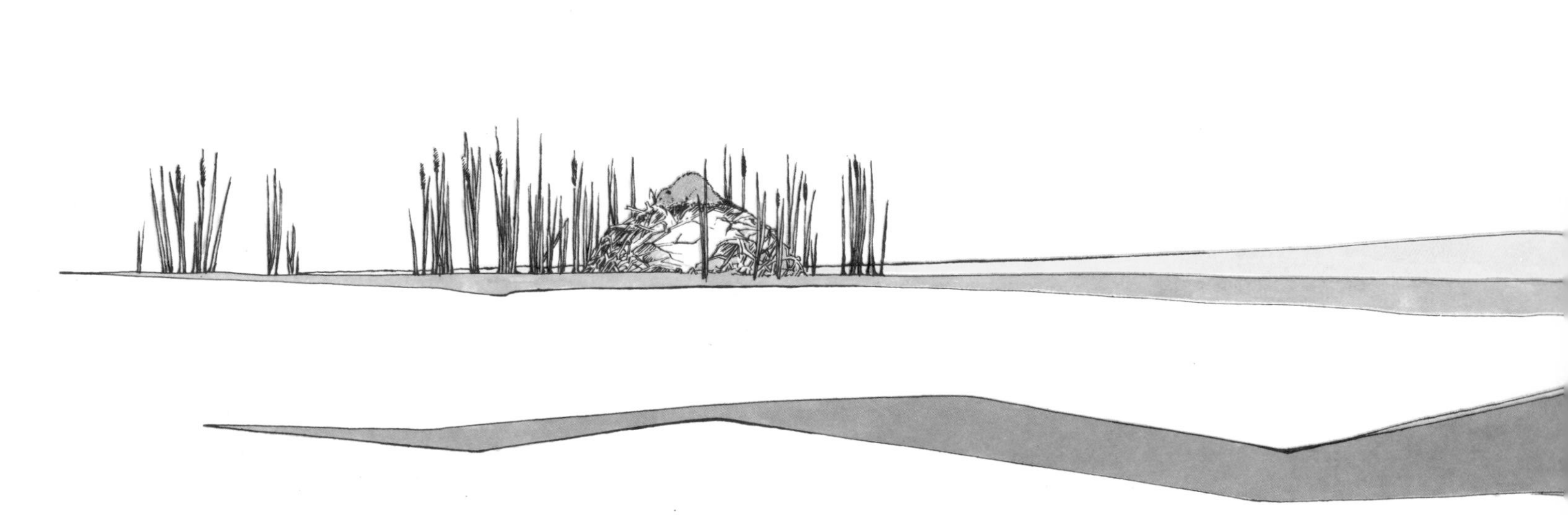

and feet so **WET.**

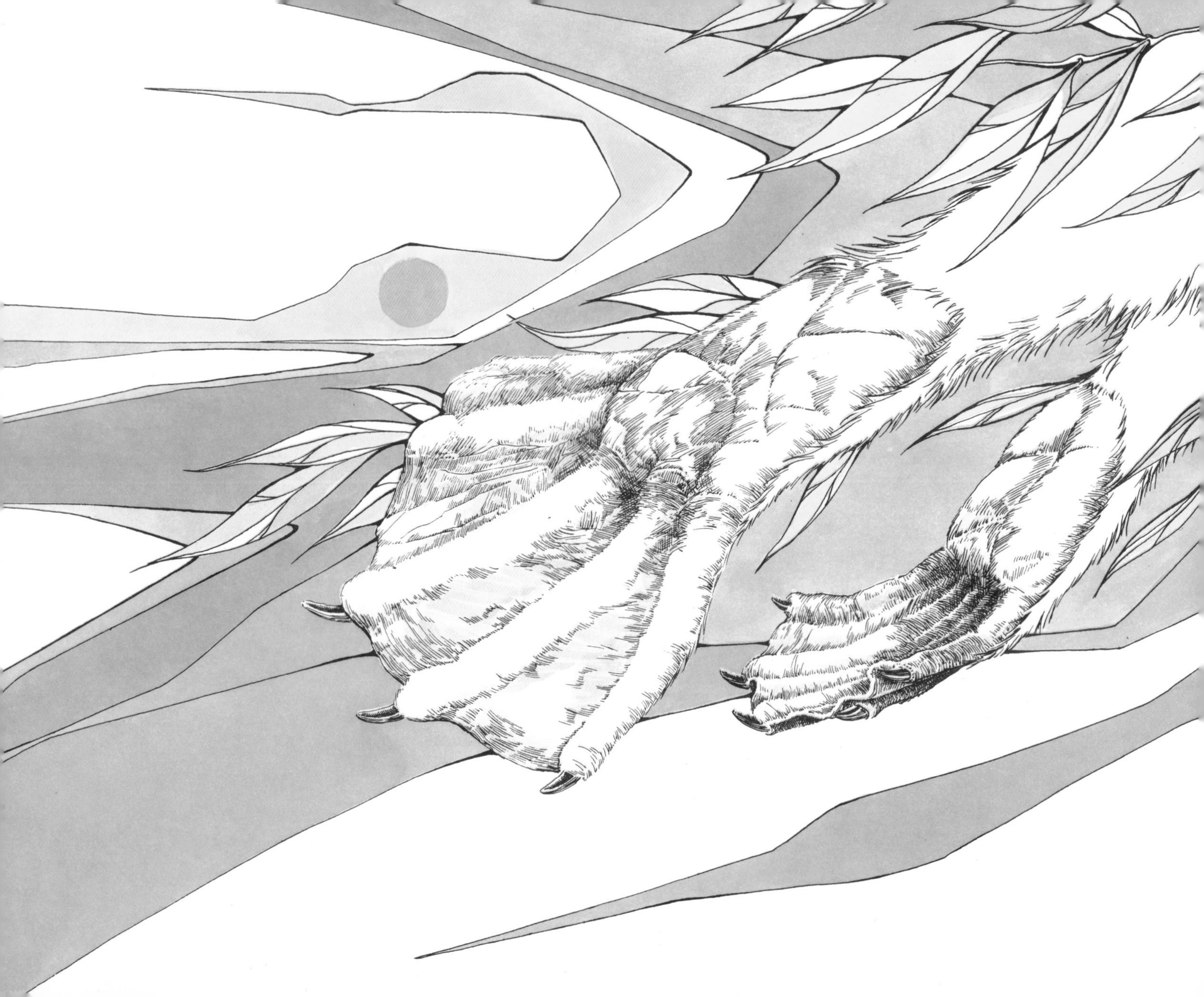

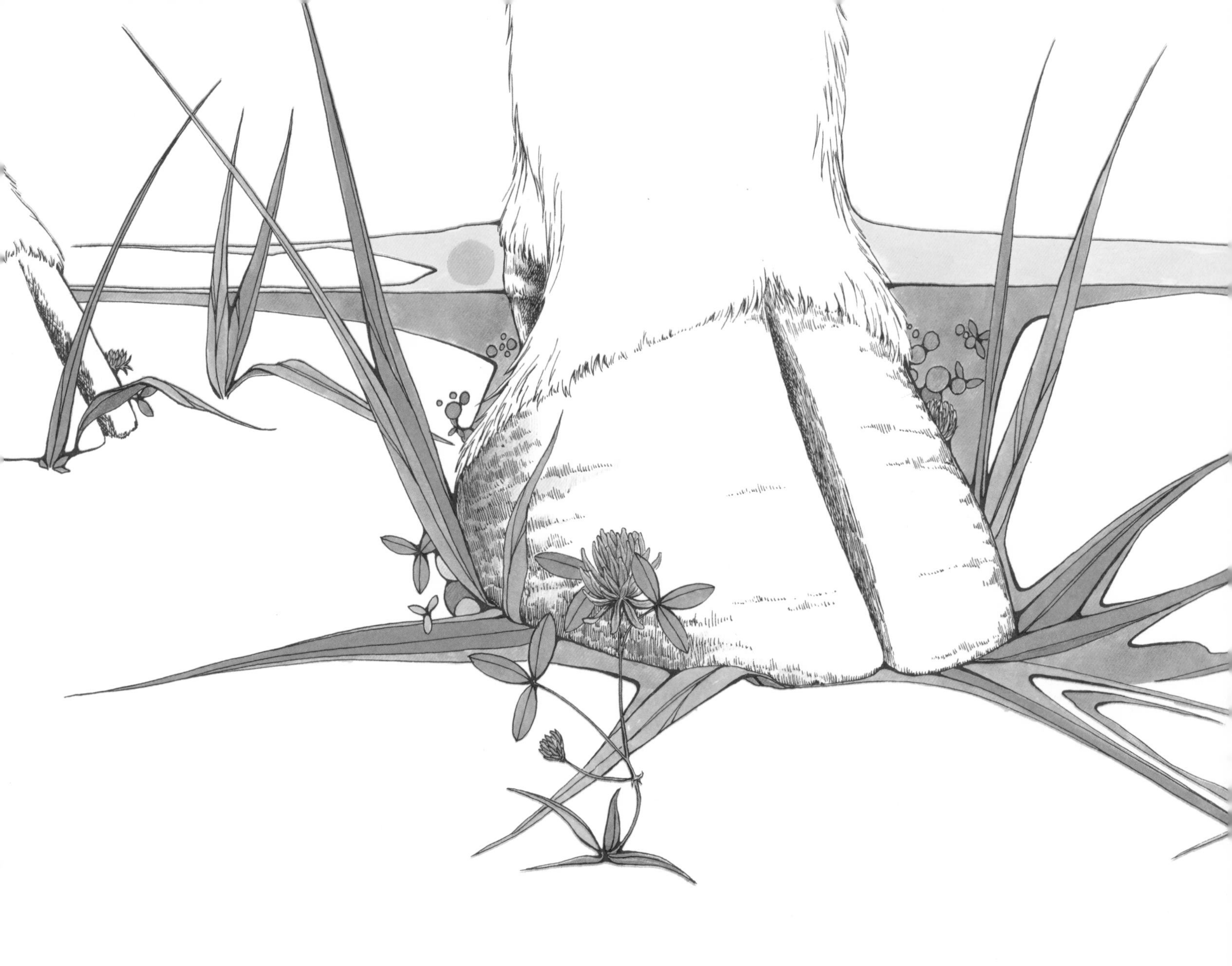

I *really* like HARD feet,

SLOW feet,

THIN feet,

DRY feet,

COOL feet,

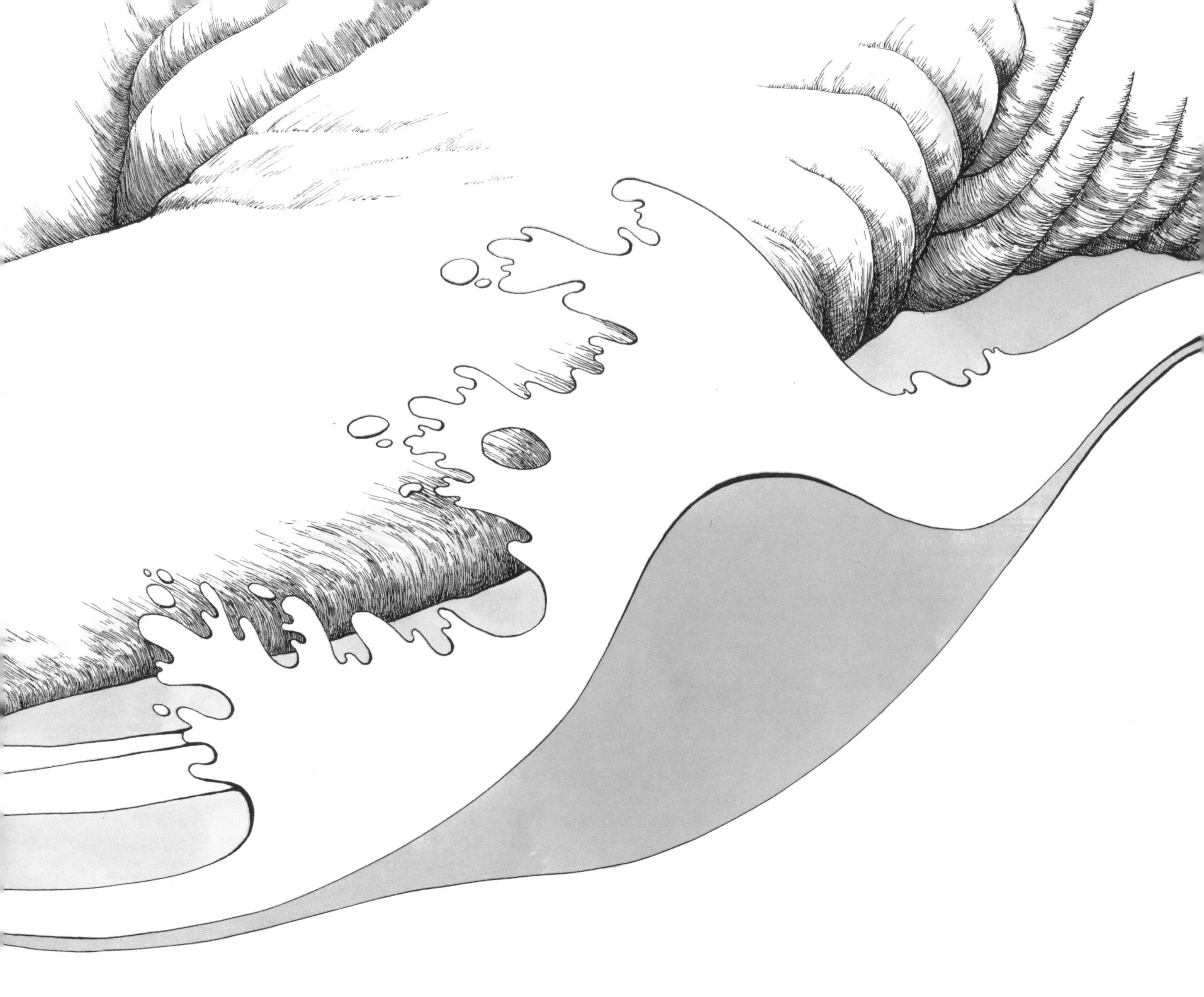

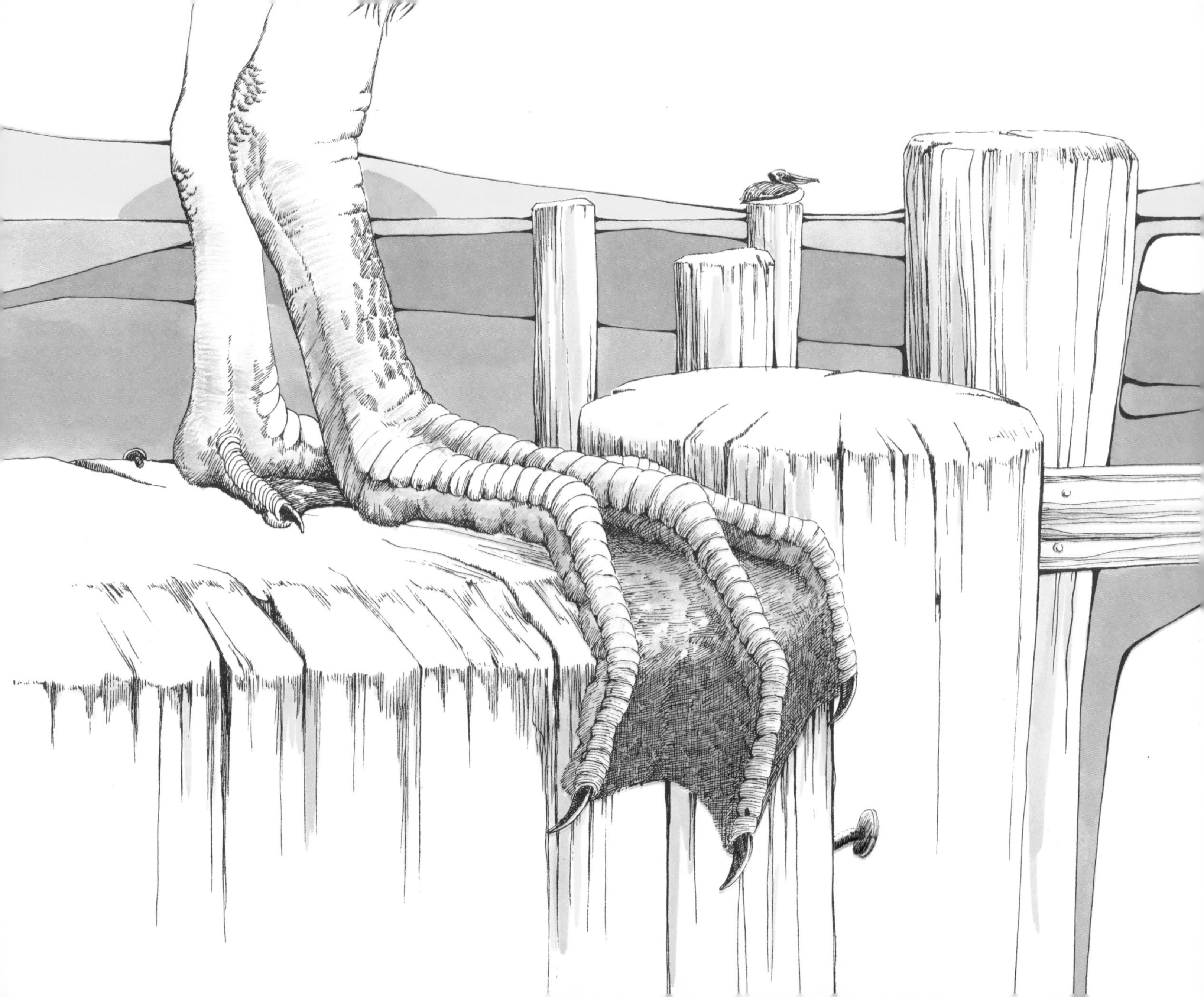

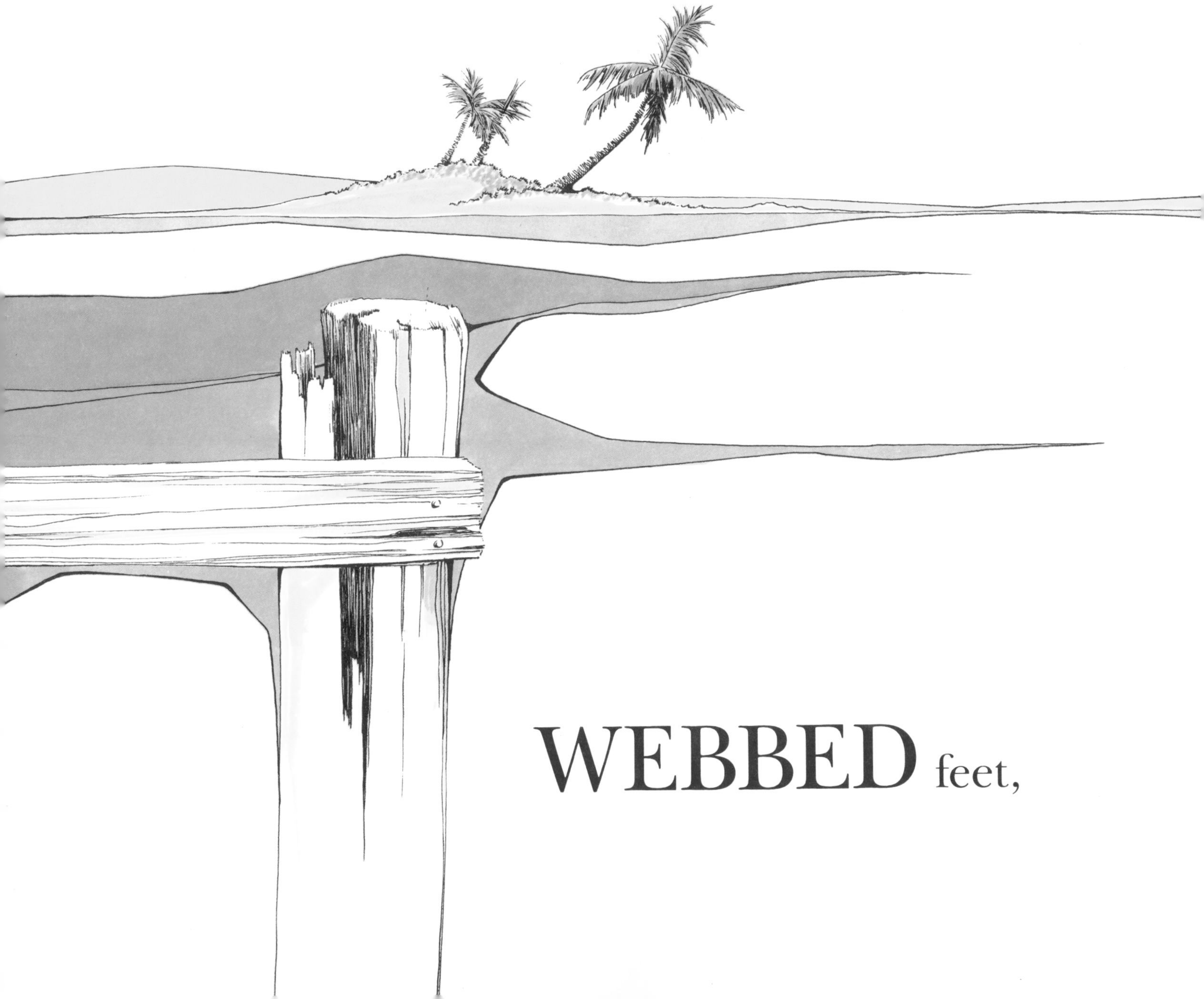

WEBBED feet,

and CLEAN feet, too!

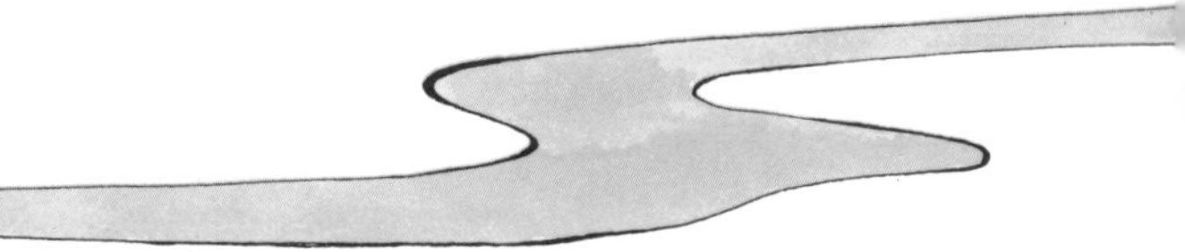

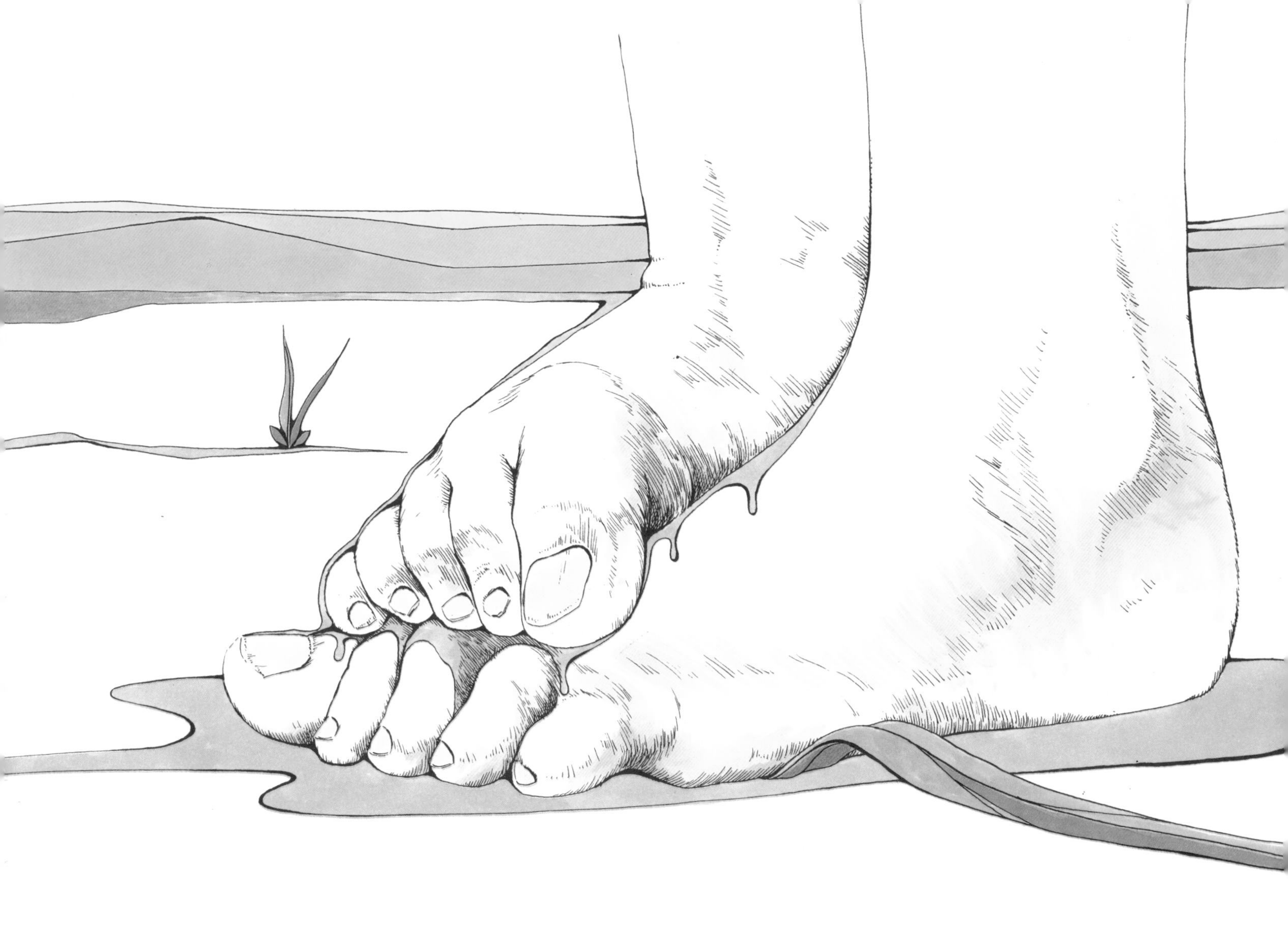

In this book you have seen the feet of the following animals.
They are listed in the order that their feet appear.

Jacket: elephant, antelope, emu, bear

Front matter: heron, emu, pygmy hippopotamus, giraffe, sloth

Text: elephant, horse, armadillo, bear, rhinoceros, beaver, bison, tortoise, heron, camel, walrus, pelican, human